D0454748

BLUE
LIPSTICK

BLUE LIPSTICK

Concrete Poems by John Grandits

Clarion Books • New York

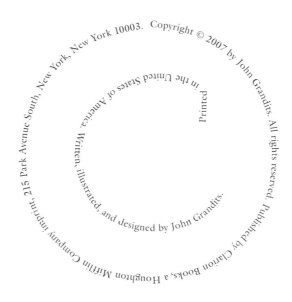
For information about permission to reproduce selections
from this book, write to Permissions, Houghton Mifflin Company,
215 Park Avenue South, New York 10003.

www.clarionbooks.com

Printed in Singapore

Library of Congress Cataloging-in-Publication Data
Grandits, John.
Blue lipstick / by John Grandits.
p. cm.
ISBN-13: 978-0-618-56860-4
ISBN-10: 0-618-56860-3
1. Concrete poetry, American. 2. Children's poetry, American. I. Title.
PS3607.R363B56 2007
811'.6–dc22   2006023332

CL ISBN-13: 978-0-618-56860-4   CL ISBN-10: 0-618-56860-3
PA ISBN-13: 978-0-618-85132-4   PA ISBN-10: 0-618-85132-1

WCP 10 9 8 7 6 5 4 3 2 1

Thanks to Joanne, Amanda and her cousin Kelsey, Signature Tracy, Mayfair Gary, Jordan & Tara, Mom & James, and my personal cheerleader, Andrea.

For
Marcia & Julianna

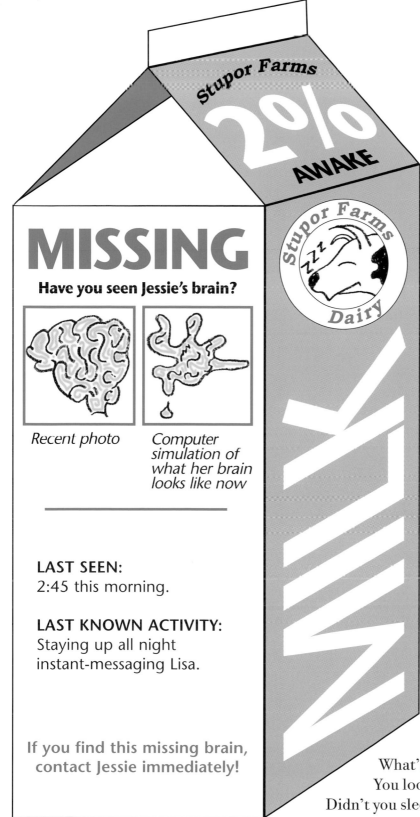

Stupor Farms

2% AWAKE

Stupor Farms
zzz
Dairy

MISSING

Have you seen Jessie's brain?

Recent photo

Computer simulation of what her brain looks like now

LAST SEEN:
2:45 this morning.

LAST KNOWN ACTIVITY:
Staying up all night instant-messaging Lisa.

If you find this missing brain, contact Jessie immediately!

MILK

Jessie,
wake up!
Eat your cereal.
What's wrong with you?
You look totally out of it.
Didn't you sleep well last night?

BAD HAIR DAY

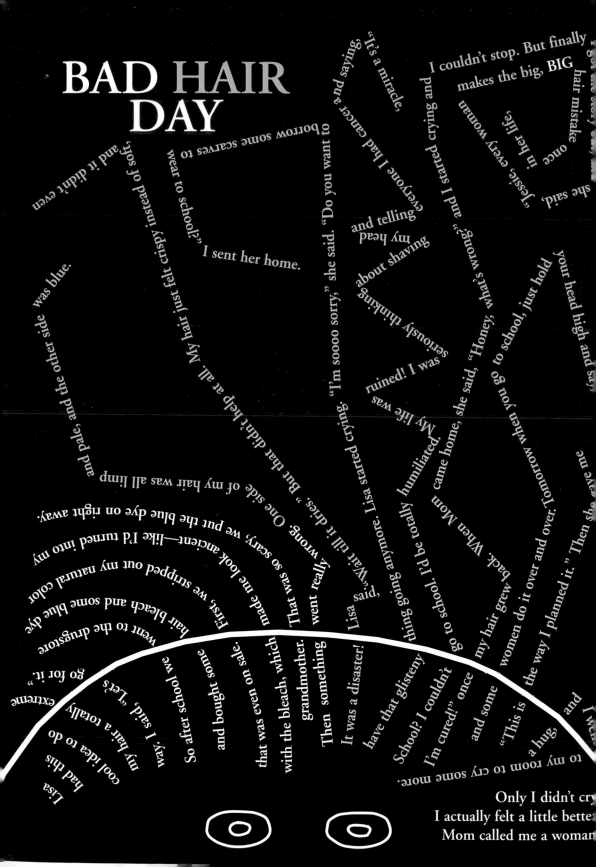

"Lisa had this cool idea to do my hair a totally extreme way," I said, "Let's go for it."

So after school we went to the drugstore and bought some hair bleach and some blue dye that was even on sale.

First, we stripped out my natural color with the bleach, which made me look ancient—like I'd turned into my grandmother. That was so scary, we put the blue dye on right away. One side of my hair was all limp and pale, and the other side was blue.

Then something went really wrong.

"Wait till it dries," Lisa said. But that didn't help at all. My hair just felt crispy instead of soft, and it didn't even have that glisteny thing going anymore.

It was a disaster! Lisa started crying. "I'm soooo sorry," she said. "Do you want to borrow some scarves to wear to school?" I sent her home.

School? I couldn't go to school. I'd be totally humiliated. My life was ruined! I was seriously thinking about shaving my head and telling everyone I had cancer.

When Mom came home, she said, "Honey, what's wrong?" and I started crying and I couldn't stop. But finally she said, "Jessie, every woman makes the big, BIG hair mistake once in her life.

"It's a miracle," and "I'm cured!" once my hair grew back. And some women do it over and over. Tomorrow when you go to school, just hold your head high and say, 'This is the way I planned it.'" Then she gave me a hug, and I went to my room to cry some more.

Only I didn't cry.
I actually felt a little better.
Mom called me a woman

The Wall

MY SIDE

Life is simpler if
you have a wall.
It keeps away
people who drag
you down, like
this girl I knew
in seventh grade.
Agnes. We were
sort of friendly.
I told her I liked
her tank top.
She insisted,
she *insisted* that I
borrow it. It sort of
got ruined.
An accident.
She insisted,
she *insisted* that I
pay her for it.
I paid her for it.
Then she forgot
I'd paid her for it.
She conveniently
forgot I'd paid!
My mother said,
"It's not worth
the grief" and went
over to Agnes's
house and paid
her mother—even
though I'd already
paid Agnes.
And that was that.
You've got to be
careful who you
make friends with.
So now I've got
this wall . . .

THE OTHER SIDE

Lisa—only
my best
friend in the
universe

Mom
and
Dad

My little
cousin
Natalie

Robert
(half of the
time)

My cat,
Boo-Boo
Kitty

Fast-food chains
that cook their
french fries in
animal fat

Smokers
(of anything)!

Talentless
12-year-old
pop stars

Rich girls who
spend more on
one pair of shoes
than I spend on
clothes in a year

Meat
eaters

Kids who cut
the cafeteria
line

Mr. Holt,
my English
teacher

People
with
totally
boring
karma

Cheerleaders

Robert
(the other half
of the time)

The school
bus driver
(yuck!)

if you're
three
years

Grown-ups
who talk
to you as

Guy
jocks

Everybody
on the
school bus,
near the
school bus,
or even
wearing
that shade
of yellow

B.*U*.R*p*.

Robert! Say "Excuse me."

What?

Say "Excuse me." When
you burp, you're supposed
to say "Excuse me."

Why?

Because that's what you do.

Right. Like you always do everything

you're supposed to do.

You always pick up your room.

You always come home

on time for dinner.

You always tell Mom and Dad

exactly where you're going

and who you're going to be with.

Yeah, yeah, yeah. Whatever.

But I always say "Excuse me"

because it's good manners.

—long pause—

Is Like
Swimming
Upstream in
a River to
Nowhere

You shut up.

No, you shut up.

No, you shut up.

You shut up.

Shut up.

Daily Heaven News.

funny pages of the

God must put that in the

That's a real laugh!

So you ask God to bless me?

"God bless you."

I'm supposed to say

Because when you sneeze,

Really? Why not?

after you sneeze.

You don't have to say, "Excuse me,"

Excuse me.

Ahhh—ch—ch—ch

Zombie Jocks

Trophy, trophy, trophy, trophy.
Zombie jocks, we want the trophy.
Trophy, trophy, give us trophy.
Give the zombie jocks the trophy.

Football, baseball, we will win 'em.
When we wrestle, we must pin 'em.
Soccer, hockey, we will skin 'em.
On our bikes, you bet we'll Schwinn 'em.

Don't like music, art, or science.
We prefer the Rams and Giants.
Don't like movies. Don't like dancing.
Don't like dating or romancing.

Trophy, trophy, trophy, trophy.
Zombie jocks must have the trophy.
Shiny, shiny, pretty trophy
With our names engraved on trophy.

PEP RALLY

Why do they force us to come to these stupid pep rallies?
I don't want to be here.
I'm not feeling peppy, and the pep rally isn't helping.
These things are only set up so that the cheerleaders can show off,
and all the boys can drool over them—
especially Andrea Herkimer.

I don't actually hate Andrea, since we've never spoken.
But if we ever *did* speak, I would hate her.

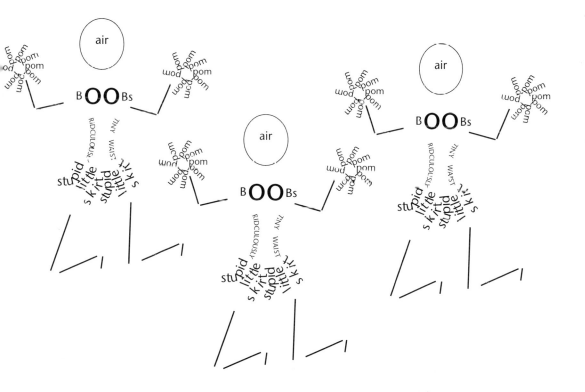

MONDRIAN

Dad and I went to the Art Institute

make ultra-cool radical art." Dad said, "It's not easy to be creative." And I thought to myself, "You wouldn't believe how creative I have to be just to get through the day." He said, "It's tough being an artist. You've got to struggle for years. People often misunderstand your work. You've got to be thick-skinned because critics can be cruel. You don't have any money. And in many ways you're really alone." And I said, "It sounds like high school."

do that when I grow up—

There was a show of work by Mondrian, and the guy totally rocks!

He did these paintings with just boxes and lines, and he only used

black and yellow and blue and red. I mean, he didn't mix his

colors at all. It was so simple and so elegant. I said, "I wish I could

Go look in the mirror!

Dad says, "You may not leave the house like that!"
and "Don't you care about your appearance at all?"
and "Just look at yourself, young lady."
He throws his hands in the air like he's seeking divine intervention.
I roll my eyes,
but I go over to the mirror.

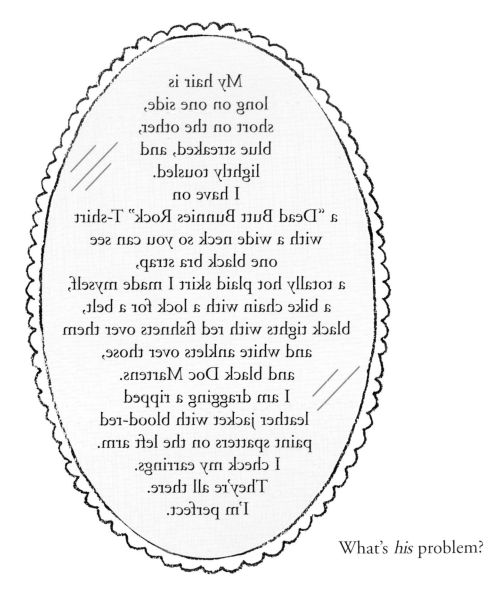

My hair is
long on one side,
short on the other,
blue streaked, and
lightly tousled.
I have on
a "Dead Butt Bunnies Rock" T-shirt
with a wide neck so you can see
one black bra strap,
a totally hot plaid skirt I made myself,
a bike chain with a lock for a belt,
black tights with red fishnets over them
and white anklets over those,
and black Doc Martens.
I am dragging a ripped
leather jacket with blood-red
paint spatters on the left arm.
I check my earrings.
They're all there.
I'm perfect.

What's *his* problem?

I went to Sylvia's Psychic Shack yesterday to get this new kind of tarot deck that has pictures of dead rock stars instead of the regular pictures. But Sylvia said she didn't carry those cards, because they might give off bad vibrations. What ever. So I was looking around, and Sylvia was talking to another customer, and the woman said, "No, I wasn't from Atlantis itself, I was from one of the small islands off Atlantis." And even though I wasn't part of the conversation, I said, "You mean, like, in a past life you lived in Atlantis?" She said, "Yeah." And I said, "And you didn't even live in town, you lived in some wanky suburb?" And she said, "Well, the schools were better." And I said, "What kind of SUVs did they drive in this suburb of Atlantis?" She acted all put out, and Sylvia gave me an evil look, but I didn't care. It just proved to me that no matter how many times they're reincarnated, some people drag their totally boring karma around with them forever.

suBURB of ATLANTiS

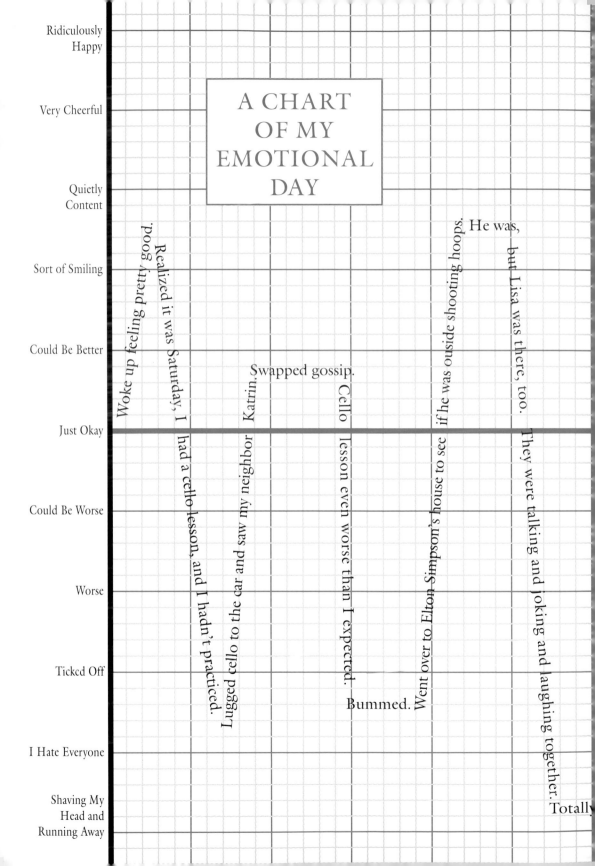

A CHART OF MY EMOTIONAL DAY

Vertical axis (top to bottom): Ridiculously Happy · Very Cheerful · Quietly Content · Sort of Smiling · Could Be Better · Just Okay · Could Be Worse · Worse · Ticked Off · I Hate Everyone · Shaving My Head and Running Away

Woke up feeling pretty good.

Realized it was Saturday, I had a cello lesson, and I hadn't practiced.

Lugged cello to the car and saw my neighbor Katrin.

Swapped gossip.

Cello lesson even worse than I expected. Bummed.

Went over to Elton Simpson's house to see if he was ouside shooting hoops. He was,

but Lisa was there, too.

They were talking and joking and laughing together. Totally

Homework. Had to come up with a stupid chart for math class.

Called Lisa. Bed.

Robert forced to eat his slice standing and glued to my door.

Found note from Mom: "No snacks this afternoon. Making tuna surprise tonight!"

He was totally defenseless. Hah!

Mom changed menu. Ordered broccoli pizza instead.

Caught my stupid younger brother trying to superglue my bedroom door shut. Stomped off to tell Dad.

Robert managed to superglue his hand to my bedroom door.

Walked home with Lisa. She said Elton kept asking about me: What I liked and what kinds of things I liked to do.

ımmed.

Science

Goofy stunts

Stupid Sports

EGO

Gross Behavior

Geekiness

Jerkiness

Sister-torturing plans

ART

Disgusting need for meat

Unnecessary insults

At lunch on Saturday,
I was telling my brother about phrenology. That's
the ancient art of reading people's personalities by examining
the bumps on their heads. He said, "Sounds like ancient
superstition to me." I said, "No, it really works." And
he said, "Prove it. Read my bumps." So I put on a good act.
I ran my hands over his scalp and said stuff like, "Your math
skills are excellent" and "You are a natural athlete" and
"Girls are attracted to you." Boy, did he eat it up! "Maybe
there's more to this than I thought," he said. Then I did
a dramatic pause. "Uh-oh," I said. And he said, "What? Tell me."
And I said, "Well, I'm afraid you'll never be a scientist. In fact, instead
of a bump in the science area, you have a dent." Of course he got
all freaked out and said that he *had* to be a scientist! It was the
only thing he'd ever wanted to be. (Like I didn't know.) So I acted
all sympathetic, and I said, "Lucky for you, there's an ancient way to
correct these things." Then I smacked him on the head with my soup spoon.
He yelped and rubbed the spot. "Feel that?" I asked. "That's your science bump.
Now you can be a famous scientist!" I smiled sweetly; then I added, "Do you want to
be a famous artist, too?" That's when he made a grab for me, and I ran to my room and
locked the door.

All My Important Thinking Gets Done in the Shower

The next time Mom and Dad go out, I could trick Robert into going down to the basement, figure out some way to block the door, and leave him there.

If I took down all the posters on my wall, I could paint a huge mural of the Seven Earth Goddesses. That would be awesome.

College! College! College! . . . Enough about college. I wonder if there's an art school that teaches you how to do tattooing and piercing.

I hate zoos. I wouldn't want to be stuck in a cage. But petting zoos are a lot of fun. I should start a petting zoo for vegetables.

Maybe I could get a job this summer. Then if I saved enough money and got my learner's permit, I could buy a motor scooter.

Football is so stupid. I bet it would be a lot less violent if the players wore tutus and ballet shoes.

Mom's tossing the laundry-room curtains because Robert got bleach on them. They would make a totally cool skirt.

Boo Boo Kitty is layin' down a mellow track.
Boo Boo Kitty is layin' it's fine.
Cat poetry! It's sweet, pepper can't come close
Even the smoooothest sound.
to the Boo Boo Kitty than any human could ever be.
She's more laid back the Buddha of poetry, and
She just sits on my lap.
purrrr, purrrppp, purrrrrppppppppppers.
Don't need speakers. Don't need earphones.
Don't need a $35 ticket.
All I gotta do is make my lap
available for the concert.

Purr Verse

I don't think I'm in love with Elton Simpson,
but . . . well . . . you know. I definitely like him.
The thing is, I don't have much to say to him.
I mean, what do guys talk about, anyway?
What am I going to say—"How about that Bears game last night?"
Not likely.

But here's the deal: Elton got into Advanced English.
I didn't.
His teacher, Mr. Fox, posted the class's required reading list.
So I'm thinking, I'll read all the books, too!
That way, when I see Elton, we can talk about them,
and we'll have this soul-revealing intellectual connection.

It took me, like, a million years to read all the books,
'cause I also had a list to get through for my English class.
But I made little notes so I could remember stuff.
Then I sort of casually bumped into Elton at school.

Me: "I've been thinking. Wasn't it funny in Tom Sawyer
         when Tom and Huck and Joe went to their own funeral?
         And everybody who hated them before was so sad?
         I'd love to go to my own funeral
         and see what people said about me! Wouldn't you?"
Elton: "Huh?"
Me: "You know, the funeral in Tom Sawyer."
Elton: Blank expression.
Me: "One of the books you have to read for Advanced English."
Elton: "Oh, I didn't bother reading those.
         I just sort of checked them out on the Internet."

So I don't have a boyfriend.
But I've read more books than all the kids in the Advanced English class
I couldn't get into.

VOLLEYBALL PRACTICE

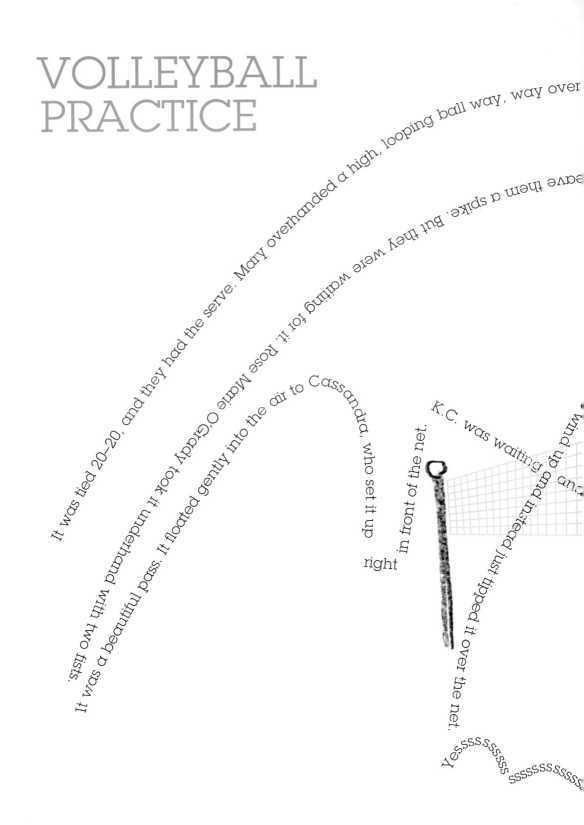

It was tied 20–20, and they had the serve. Mary overhanded a high, looping ball way, way over ...ave them a spike. But they were waiting for it. Rose Marie O'Grady took it underhand with two fists. It was a beautiful pass. It floated gently into the air to Cassandra, who set it up right in front of the net. K.C. was waiting and ...ind up and instead just tipped it over the net. Yessssssssssss ssssssssssss the net and deep into our backcourt. A defensive serve. Not a tough serve to return. It just depended on what we did with it.

Patty got it and put up a nice little set to LaShondra.

LaShondra sort of freaked and sent a long ball back over the net. At least she didn't

So I pretended

They were waiting.

herself and put up a beautiful set. It was high and ready for me to slam

LaShondra redeemed

slammed it. It was a bullet. But

ssss!

Once again, brains win out over brawn.

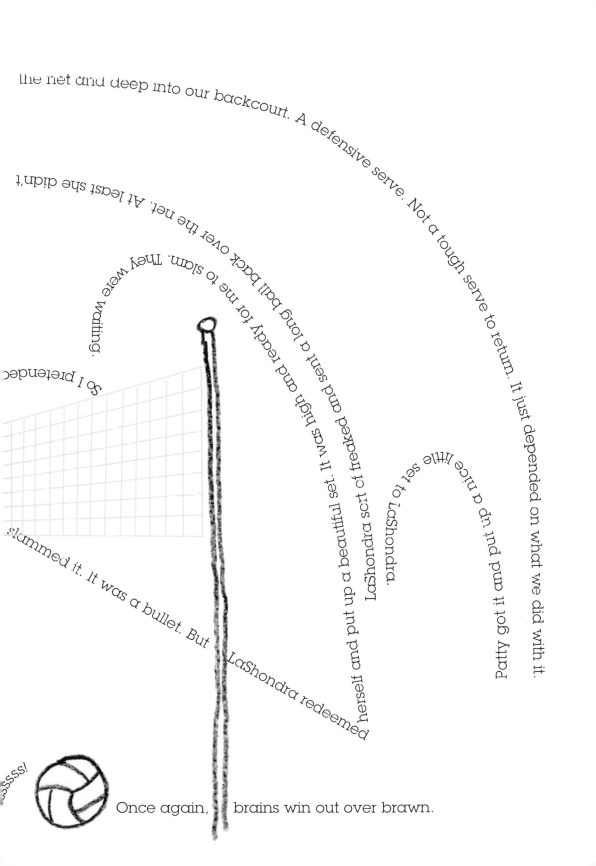

Style? Yeah, I'd love to have my own signature style. Not something preppy or conventional. Something interesting that says ME.

The kind of style that would make a guy look at me and think, "Hey, that's a girl I'd like to hang out with." Sort of post-punk urban too-cool-to-go-to-the-mall style.

But do you know what style costs? It's unbelievable. I was in this trendy boutique yesterday called Stink. Poofy rainbow skirt, $150. Tank top, $85. Color-washed jeans, $139. Cropped jean jacket, $130. Embroidered "Rock Star" T-shirt, $268! Studded dog-collar necklace, $60.

Who can afford this kind of stuff? I'm a kid. I'm not a hip-hop star. So I make some of my own clothes and shop for what's cheap and unusual and hope that it makes me look interesting. But I have the feeling that when guys see me, they're not thinking "style," they're thinking "weird."

The H-U-P Song

I babysit for my little cousin Natalie all the time.
She's great! But her mom, my Aunt Sophie, is kind of a pain.
Natalie has to be in the best preschool.
Natalie has to have the latest toys and the fanciest clothes.
Natalie can't watch TV because she might hear the word "stupid."
But that's not Natalie's fault. She's great.

So last week I was babysitting Natalie, and we were singing songs.
I said, "Let's sing the ABC song. Do you know your letters?"
And she said, "Well, I know them, but I only know them mixed up."

So we made up a song of our own.

You can imagine how proud Aunt Sophie was.

A+

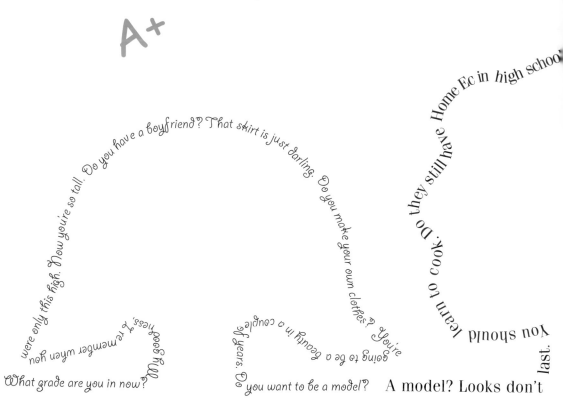

Goodness, I remember when you were only this high. Now you're so tall. Do you have a boyfriend? That skirt is just darling. Do you make your own clothes? You're going to be a beauty in a couple of years. Do you want to be a model? A model? Looks don't last. You should learn to cook. Do they still have Home Ec in high school?

What grade are you in now?

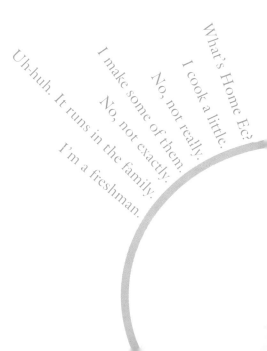

What's Home Ec?

I cook a little.

No, not really.

I make some of them.

No, not exactly.

Uh-huh. It runs in the family.

I'm a freshman.

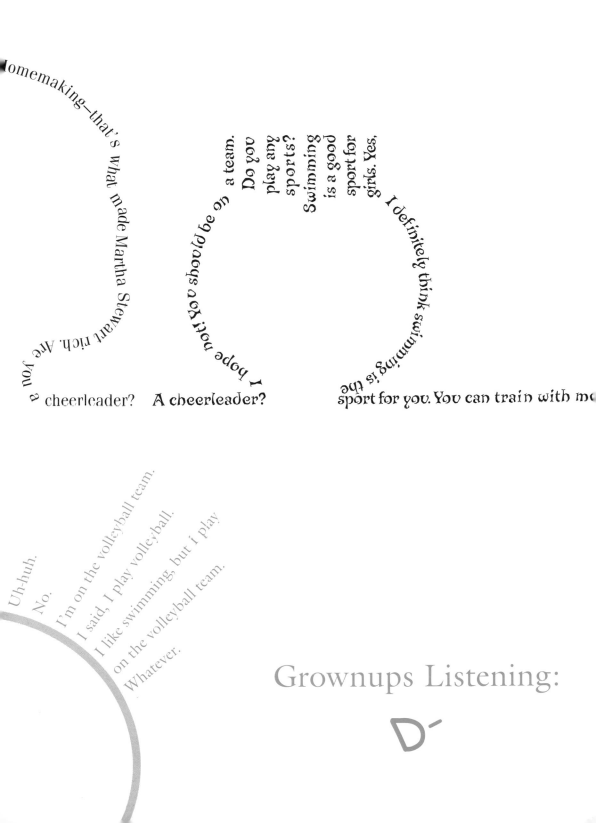

Homemaking—that's what made Martha Stewart rich. Are you a cheerleader? A cheerleader?

I hope not! You should be on a team. Do you play any sports? Swimming is a good sport for girls. Yes, I definitely think swimming is the sport for you. You can train with me

Uh-huh.

No.

I'm on the volleyball team.

I said, I play volleyball.

I like swimming, but i play on the volleyball team.

Whatever.

Grownups Listening:

D-

Angels

HALO HALO HALO HALO HALO

Bountiful blessings Devoted attention Remarkable results
Unconditiional love Good news
Glorious visions Celestial dreams Rare opportunities
Unexplained kindness Rapturous experiences
Caring gestures
Spiritual guidance
Divine intervention Mystical messages
Magical moments
Sublime happiness
Triumphant truth

Unconditional forgivenss
Friendly attitudes Good will
Metaphysical mysteries Unconditional
Helpful advice Unusual tolera
Surprising consideration
Heavenly rewards
Charitable actions
Gentle reminders Compassionate concern
Tender mercy Astonishing eve
Sympathetic though
Favorable reviews Amazing grace
Unexpected tenderness

I know guardian angels exist. I've seen some *unbelievable* things, and that's the only explanation. Robert says no way. He says it's either coincidence or the work of aliens that secretly live among us. But I know I'm right, and I've got proof. Like this time in phys. ed., Lisa is climbing the knotted rope, and she's nearly at the top, and then she loses it. So she's falling, like, a mile straight down, and Ms. Kaufman just happens to be standing there and—get this—catches her! That's the work of a smart angel. Another time, Michael Workman, the dork, is showing off in the school parking lot and almost gets creamed by a toilet-paper delivery truck. I swear, it looks like someone pushes him out of the way at the last second. But there's no one there! Now that's a stupid angel. The world would be a better place with Michael Workman in a full body cast for a year or two. But still, it's evidence: Guardian angels really exist. There's no way that aliens live among us. Unless Robert is one of them.

The Bowling Party

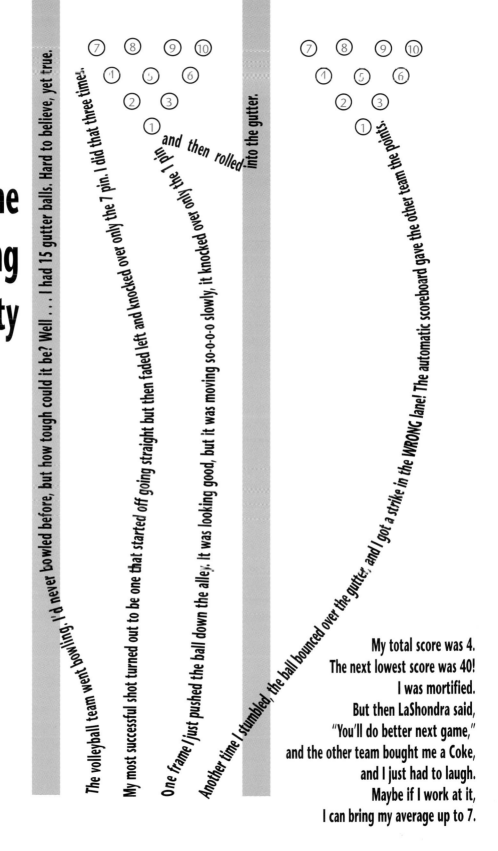

The volleyball team went bowling. I'd never bowled before, but how tough could it be? Well . . . I had 15 gutter balls. Hard to believe, yet true.

My most successful shot turned out to be one that started off going straight but then faded left and knocked over only the 7 pin. I did that three times!

One frame I just pushed the ball down the alley; it was looking good, but it was moving so-o-o-o slowly, it knocked over only the 1 pin and then rolled into the gutter.

Another time I stumbled, the ball bounced over the gutter, and I got a strike in the WRONG lane! The automatic scoreboard gave the other team the points.

My total score was 4.
The next lowest score was 40!
I was mortified.
But then LaShondra said,
"You'll do better next game,"
and the other team bought me a Coke,
and I just had to laugh.
Maybe if I work at it,
I can bring my average up to 7.

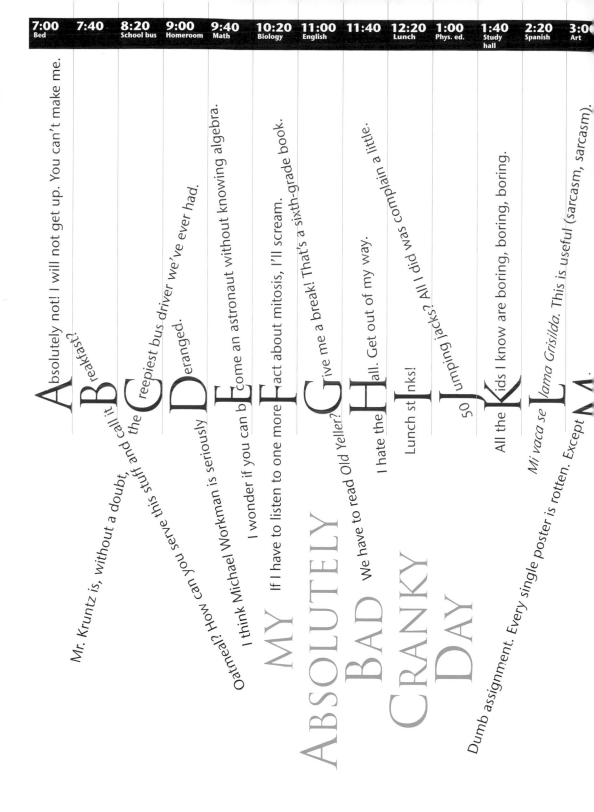

MY ABSOLUTELY BAD CRANKY DAY

Absolutely not! I will not get up. You can't make me.

Breakfast? Oatmeal? How can you serve this stuff and call it breakfast?

Creepiest bus driver we've ever had. Mr. Kruntz is, without a doubt, the creepiest bus driver we've ever had.

Deranged. I think Michael Workman is seriously deranged.

Ecome an astronaut without knowing algebra. I wonder if you can become an astronaut without knowing algebra.

Fact about mitosis, I'll scream. If I have to listen to one more fact about mitosis, I'll scream.

Give me a break! That's a sixth-grade book. We have to read Old Yeller?

Hall. Get out of my way. I hate the hall. Get out of my way.

I Lunch stinks!

Jumping jacks? All I did was complain a little. 50 jumping jacks? All I did was complain a little.

Kids I know are boring, boring, boring. All the kids I know are boring, boring, boring.

Llama Grisilda. This is useful (sarcasm, sarcasm). Mi vaca se llama Grisilda.

M. Dumb assignment. Every single poster is rotten. Except M...

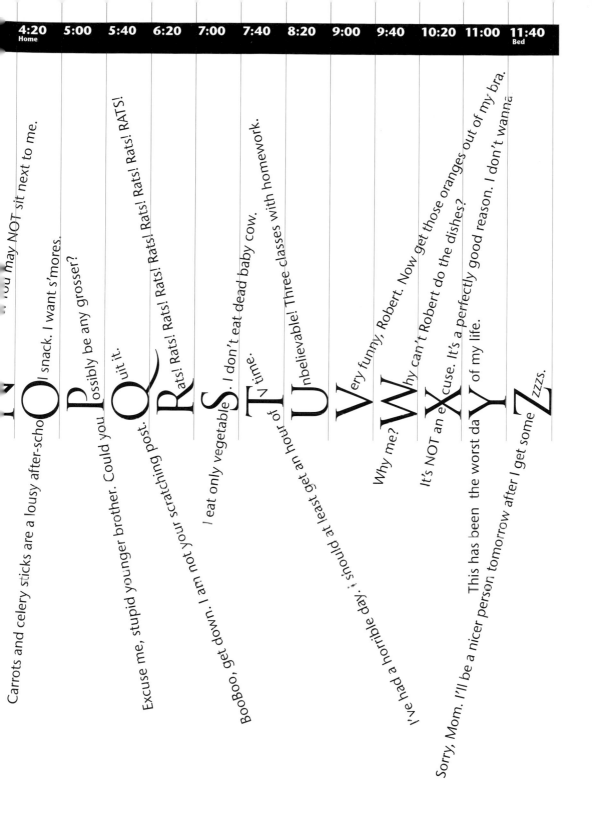

4:20 Home 5:00 5:40 6:20 7:00 7:40 8:20 9:00 9:40 10:20 11:00 11:40 Bed

...ou may NOT sit next to me.

O I snack. I want s'mores.

P ossibly be any grosser?

Q uit it.

R ats! Rats! Rats! Rats! Rats! Rats! Rats! RATS!

S . I don't eat dead baby cow.

T V time.

U nbelievable! Three classes with homework.

V ery funny, Robert. Now get those oranges out of my bra.

W hy can't Robert do the dishes?

X cuse. It's a perfectly good reason. I don't wanna

Y of my life.

Z ZZZs.

Carrots and celery sticks are a lousy after-scho

Excuse me, stupid younger brother. Could you

I eat only vegetable

BooBoo, get down.. I am not your scratching post.

I should at least get an hour of

I've had a horrible day.

Why me?

It's NOT an e

Sorry, Mom. I'll be a nicer person tomorrow after I get some

This has been the worst da

Totally Lame
English Assignment #19:
Create a series of four
to six haiku centered
on a single theme.

Eau de
School Bus Driver
in the A.M.

Garbage and garlic.
Where does he eat his breakfast?
The Trash Can Diner?

Attar de
Girls' Bathroom
During a Dance

Breath mints. Bubble gum.
Jealousy, lies, and gossip.
Ninth-grade witches' brew.

L'aire du
Michael Workman

Overbearing jerk.
Cigarette breath and B.O.
I smell him coming.

Eau de
School Bus Driver
in the P.M.

Skunk flesh on his shirt.
He's been rolling in road kill.
That explains a lot.

Essence of
Lunchroom

Mysterious meats.
Questionable vegetables.
Mix, bake, burn, and serve.

AROMA DU
FART

Wrinkle up your nose.
Turn your head from side to side.
Pretend it's not you.

Girls
We have the solution!

Feeling low?
Unattractive?
Unsure of yourself?
Unable to compete?

For as little as $5 a week, we'll make you feel good about yourself, **and other people will think you're terrific, too!**

Here's how it works:

Twice a day, one of us will come up to you and compliment you. Picture yourself in the hall with your friends, and Jessie walks up and says, "Wow, your hair looks great. Did you do something new with it?"

Or imagine yourself on the bus, and Lisa hands you some papers and says, "Thanks for loaning me your history homework. You are soooo smart!"

Prices: $5 for any one category, $2 for each additional category. Just choose from the following:

☐ Clothing ("Great skirt. I wish I could find stuff that cool.")
☐ Hair ("Your new haircut is soooo cute. Where did you get it done?")
☐ General beauty ("Do you have to look good every day? Give the rest of us a break!")
☐ Sports ("Awesome serve. You're going to be the next team captain.")
☐ Intelligence (check two)
    ☐ Science ("You're going to be the next Einstein, except without the big hair.")
    ☐ Math ("I can't believe you're doing calculus already.")
    ☐ Creative writing ("That poem you wrote was soooo sad, I cried.")
☐ Art ("You draw really well. Would you do my portrait?")

OUR GUARANTEE*
• No ironic tone of voice
• No sarcastic looks
• No behind-your-back denials
*Unless you don't pay.

SPECIAL
Sign up before Friday, and we'll say nice things about you in front of the boy of your choice!

Contact: Jessie or Lisa at locker #154 or #177

My mother says to me, "No! I will not give you a ride to school. It's only a mile. Walk." So I calmly explain to her—well, sort of calmly—that I really, really need a ride because I have an early volleyball practice, and if I walk, I might get there late. And I've just taken a shower, and my hair is still wet, and I didn't know it was going to be twenty degrees today, I could get pneumonia. Besides, I promised Lisa I'd loan her my earrings, and she absolutely has to... has to have them first thing this morning, so I need to drop them off at her house on the way. And it would be really nice if we could swing by the deli so I could get a hot cocoa because it's freezing out. Then, since we'll be in the car anyway, we can pick up some of the girls on the team, because I sort of already told them we would. Okay, okay. It's a lot of detours, and I know from geometry class that the shortest distance between point A and point B is a straight line. But what can I say? My life is more complicated than geometry.

Allergic to Time

I got a watch for my birthday. It was silver, and it had cool numbers. I wore it for a week; then it suddenly died. The guy at the repair shop said, "Some people just give off a chemical that stops watches." After that, my alarm clock started acting weird. It refused to buzz, so Dad had to get me up for school. Then three days ago, Mom got me a pendant watch.

It's beautiful—with little zirconium bits to mark the hours. But yesterday I felt this strange itch, and when I went to the girls' room, I saw that I had a rash right under the pendant. I took it off (duh!) and washed the spot. So I totally missed the school bus and got a big lecture from the parents about responsibility and taking charge of my life. But then Robert said, "Jeez, give her a break. It's not like she can help it." And Dad said, "What do you mean, Robert?" in that official parent sort of voice. And Robert said, "Don't you get it? Time hates Jessie. She'll never be on time. She'll always be late. It's just the way she is. It's like she has an allergy." There was a long silence while everybody thought about this. Finally, Dad said, "Well, that's a good point, Robert. But Jessie, at least make an effort in the future." And I will. I will also try to do something nice, but not obviously nice, for my not-always-stupid younger brother.

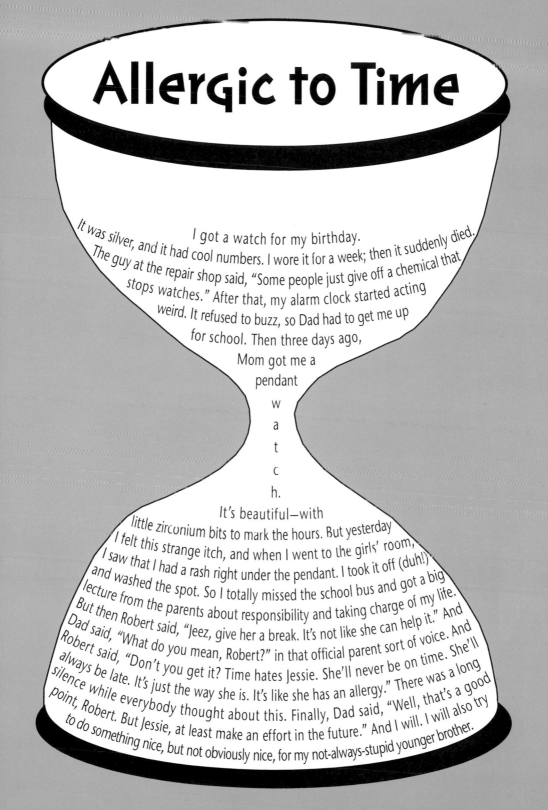

SILVER SPANDEX

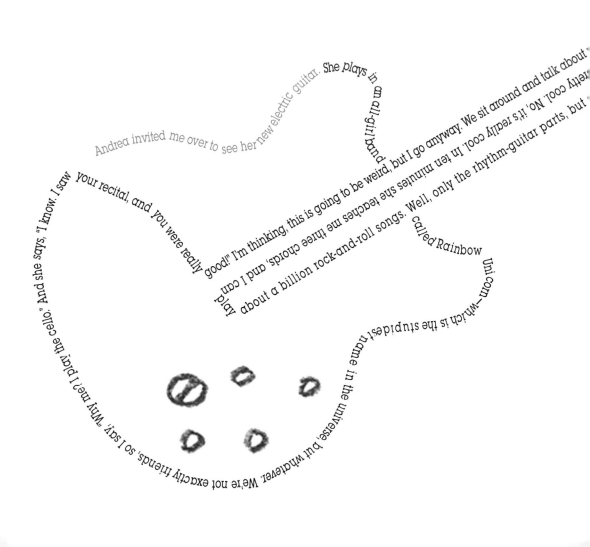

Andrea invited me over to see her new electric guitar. She plays in an all-girl band called Rainbow Unicorn—which is the stupidest name in the universe, but whatever. We're not exactly friends, so I say, "Why me? I play the cello." And she says, "I know, I saw your recital, and you were really good!" I'm thinking, this is going to be weird, but I go anyway. We sit around and talk about pretty cool. No, it's really cool. In ten minutes she teaches me three chords, and I can play about a billion rock-and-roll songs. Well, only the rhythm-guitar parts, but

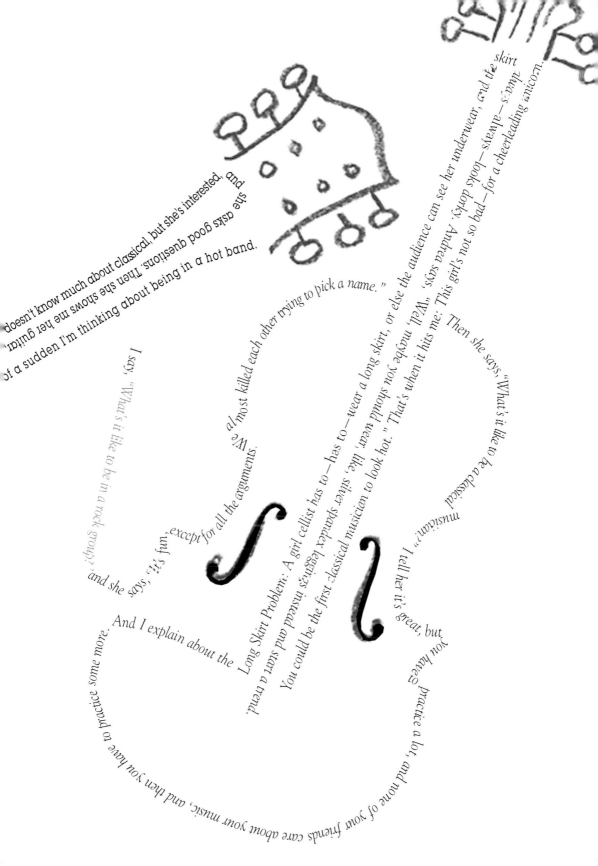

...doesn't know much about classical, but she's interested, and she asks good questions. Then she shows me her guitar. ...of a sudden I'm thinking about being in a hot band.

"What's it like to be in a rock group?" I say, and she says, "It's fun, except for all the arguments. We almost killed each other trying to pick a name."

And I explain about the Long Skirt Problem: A girl cellist has to—has to—wear a long skirt, or else the audience can see her underwear, and the skirt always—always—looks dorky. Andrea says, "Well, maybe you should wear, like, silver spandex leggings instead and start a trend. You could be the first classical musician to look hot." That's when it hits me: This girl's not so bad—for a cheerleading unicorn.

Then she says, "What's it like to be a classical musician?" I tell her it's great, but you have to practice a lot, and none of your friends care about your music, and then you have to practice some more.

The Name-Your-Rock-Band Chart

Your band will have 3,551 arguments before you break up
in an explosion of jealousy and anger. Avoid the first big fight—
choosing the band's name.
Pick one from each column.

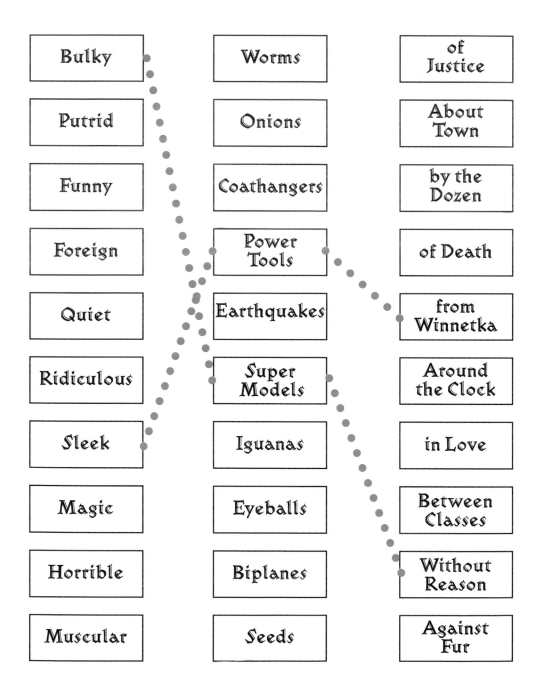

Bulky	Worms	of Justice
Putrid	Onions	About Town
Funny	Coathangers	by the Dozen
Foreign	Power Tools	of Death
Quiet	Earthquakes	from Winnetka
Ridiculous	Super Models	Around the Clock
Sleek	Iguanas	in Love
Magic	Eyeballs	Between Classes
Horrible	Biplanes	Without Reason
Muscular	Seeds	Against Fur

Tattoo
and Tongue Stud

I walk into the kitchen. Robert is at the table, eating ice cream. I sit down beside him and casually push up my sleeve so he'll see it: My new tattoo. It says, "Sex, Drugs, & Rock 'n' Roll" in spiky goth letters. "What the heck is that?" he screams. I smile. This is working out just fine. "It'th a tattoo," I say, all innocent-like. "What's wrong with you?" he demands. "Why are you lisping?" I stick out my tongue, and there it is: a perfect little silver stud, right in the center. Robert starts pumping his arm like he just won a million bucks. "Yesssss! You are in soooo much trouble," he says. "Wait till Mom and Dad see this. Dad will kill you, and then Mom   will ground you for life." I give him a big   yawn. "Who care'th?" I say. "You will, when   I tell them," he says. "They're at the neighbors', and I'm going to go get them." He takes off, and I can hear him yelling, "Mom! Dad!" all the way down the street. How perfect is this? I slide off the magnetic tongue stud. I wash off the temporary tattoo. And while I wait for my parents to come rushing home, I practice saying, "I don't know what Robert is talking about. Maybe he needs counseling." This is going to be great.

HOW I TAUGHT MY

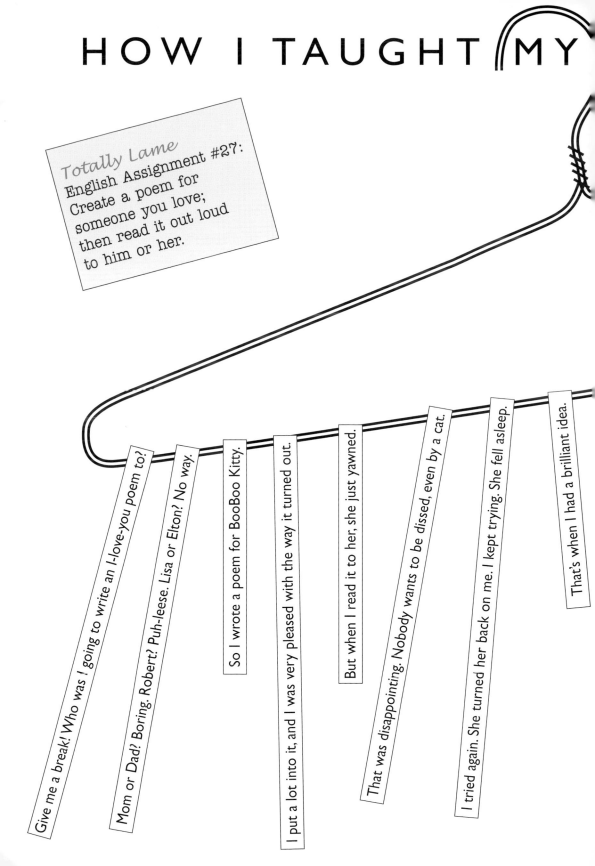

Totally Lame
English Assignment #27:
Create a poem for someone you love; then read it out loud to him or her.

Give me a break! Who was I going to write an I-love-you poem to?

Mom or Dad? Boring. Robert? Puh-leese. Lisa or Elton? No way.

So I wrote a poem for BooBoo Kitty.

I put a lot into it, and I was very pleased with the way it turned out.

But when I read it to her, she just yawned.

That was disappointing. Nobody wants to be dissed, even by a cat.

I tried again. She turned her back on me. I kept trying. She fell asleep.

That's when I had a brilliant idea.

CAT TO LOVE POETRY

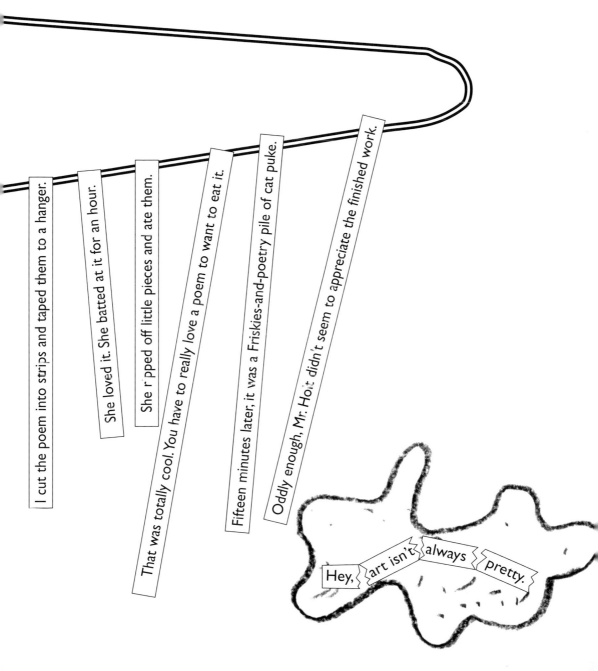

I cut the poem into strips and taped them to a hanger.

She loved it. She batted at it for an hour.

She r pped off little pieces and ate them.

That was totally cool. You have to really love a poem to want to eat it.

Fifteen minutes later, it was a Friskies-and-poetry pile of cat puke.

Oddly enough, Mr. Holt didn't seem to appreciate the finished work.

Hey, art isn't always pretty.

The Secret

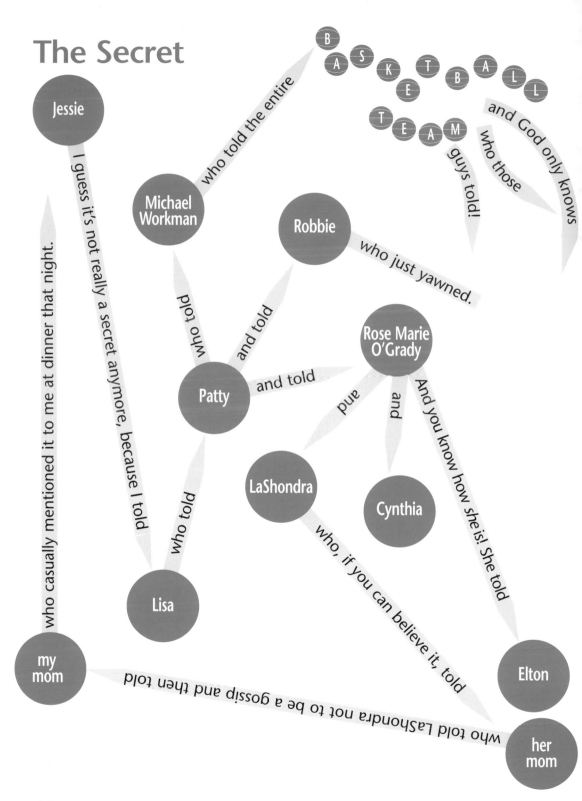

Jessie

BASKETBALL TEAM

who told the entire

and God only knows

who those

guys told!

Michael Workman

Robbie

who just yawned.

who told

and told

Rose Marie O'Grady

Patty

and told

and

and

And you know how she is! She told

LaShondra

Cynthia

who told

Lisa

who, if you can believe it, told

Elton

I guess it's not really a secret anymore, because I told

who casually mentioned it to me at dinner that night.

my mom

who told LaShondra not to be a gossip and then told

her mom

Now everybody knows. I just wish I could remember who told me.

Happy B*day, Mom

Dad gave Mom the coolest gift:
a hot-air balloon ride—
and we all got to go! I couldn't wait.
I've always wanted to float through the air
in a beautiful balloon.

On the way there, I teased Robert unmercifully.
I told him that he was too little to ride with us,
that they wouldn't let a kid his age go
because he'd get sick or be scared or fall out.

But they let Robert on, and there we were,
swinging and floating
and swinging and floating and
just as we were swinging over some
rich guy's absolutely beautiful swimming pool . . .
            I lost it.

HOT-AIR BALLOON

I'll never hear the end of this.

Barf Barf

Barf Barf Barf Barf Barf

The Wall
(Revisited)

I started taking down my wall this year. Mom said, "Maybe you're maturing." Yeah? Then why can't I get a motorbike? Dad said, "Maybe you're learning to get along with people." That made me mad. "Are you saying I didn't get along with people before?" I yelled. "I've *always* gotten along with everybody! They just haven't gotten along with me." Dad said, "Okay, okay. You win. I was wrong." And he went back to reading his book. Robert said, "You are a noble adversary, O Evil One. Yet soon my powers will defeat you." What an idiot. Anyway, I still have a wall. But now I've got more company.

BooBoo Kitty

Elton Simpson, even though the boyfriend thing seems unlikely

The girls on the volleyball team

Robert (when he's not around)

Mom and Dad

My little cousin Natalie

Andrea, a cheerleader who turned out to be a regular person— annoyingly pretty, but a regular person

Lisa forever

Meat eaters

Robert (when he is around)

90% of the kids on the school bus

Mr. Holt, my English teacher

Smokers

Guy jocks

The school bus driver (It's more than the B.O. He's got issues.)

I mean, a girl's got to have *some* standards.

Pocket
Poem

It's a good idea to carry a poem in your pocket
in case of an emotional emergency.

Sometimes I carry around "The Cremation of Sam McGee."
It's guaranteed to cheer me up. I don't know why.
At the end, Sam freezes to death and makes a ghostly appearance.
It sends a chill through me. But I always feel better.

Some days I need a sonnet.
When Shakespeare writes to a faraway girlfriend,
he writes what I wish I could write:
"For thy sweet love remember'd such wealth brings
That then I scorn to change my state with kings."

And some days only a silly little kid's poem will do.
"A tree toad loved a she-toad, who lived up in a tree.
He was a two-toed tree toad, but a three-toed toad was she."
You've got to smile when you read that.

Yes, it's a good idea to carry a poem in your pocket.
It's a little snack for your soul.

These poems were written on a Macintosh G4 using QuarkXPress Software. The drawings were done with a Bristol China Marker and touched up in Adobe Photoshop.
The poems are set in the following typefaces:

Airstream ITC
American Typewriter
Angryhog ITC
Arial Black
Belch
Bembo
Blackmoor
Bodoni ITC
(Bodoni Ornaments)
Bookman Old Style
Brainhead
Caflisch Script
Caslon
Centaur
CHARLEMAGNE
Clover ITC
Comic Sans
Courier New
Django ITC
Ibola
Fenice ITC
Galliard ITC
Adobe Garamond
Giddyup
Gill Sans Condensed
Goudy Old Style
Goudy Text

Grapefruit ITC
Harlequin
Jiggery Pokery ITC
Jott
Kaufmann
Kristen Normal ITC
Kumquat ITC
Lingo ITC
Lubalin Graph
Lucida Handwriting
Lvcifers Penſion
Ludwig ITC
Marker Felt
Medici Script
Pesto
Regular Joe
Sand
Sloppy Joe
(Sonata)
Stone Informal
Stone Sans
Tapioca ITC
Tempus
TRAJAN
Uncle Stinky
Werkstatt Engraved
(Zapf Dingbats)